Contents

Look at Me!	4-5
Our House	6-7
Off to School	8-9
Our Classroom	10-11
Colour Fun	12-13
When I Grow Up	14-15
Long Time Ago	16-17

Busy Shopping	18-19
Monster Lunch	20-21
Time to Play	22-23
On the Farm	24-25
At the Beach	26-27

Birthday Party	28-29
Animal Magic	30-31
In the Bath	32-33
Time for Bed	34-35
My ABC	36-37
Count 123	38-39
Shapes	40-41
Opposites	42-43
Weather	44
Time	45
Index	46-47

Look at Me!

chest

leg

foot

toe

back

elbow

bottom

finger

tummy

knee

hand

hair

arm

head

shoulders

My First OXFORD Book of Words

Illustrated by David Melling
Compiled by Neil Morris

OXFORD
UNIVERSITY PRESS

For Bosiljka, Branko and Igor Sunajko.
D.M.

OXFORD
UNIVERSITY PRESS

Great Clarendon Street, Oxford OX2 6DP

Oxford New York

Athens Auckland Bangkok Bogotá Buenos Aires Calcutta
Cape Town Chennai Dar es Salaam Delhi Florence Hong Kong Istanbul
Karachi Kuala Lumpur Madrid Melbourne Mexico City Mumbai
Nairobi Paris São Paulo Singapore Taipei Tokyo Toronto Warsaw
and associated companies in Berlin Ibadan

Oxford is a registered trade mark of Oxford University Press

Illustrations copyright © David Melling 1999
Text copyright © Oxford University Press 1999

First published in hardback 1999
First published in paperback 2000

1 3 5 7 9 10 8 6 4 2

British Library Cataloguing in Publication Data
Data available

ISBN 0–19–910745–9

Printed in Italy

face

cheek

ear

eye

chin

mouth

teeth

tongue

neck

nose

girl

boy

5

Our House

roof

dustbin

gate

stairs

chimney

fence

garage

window

door

dog

cat

rabbit

spider

snail

letters

post bag

leaf

flower

tree

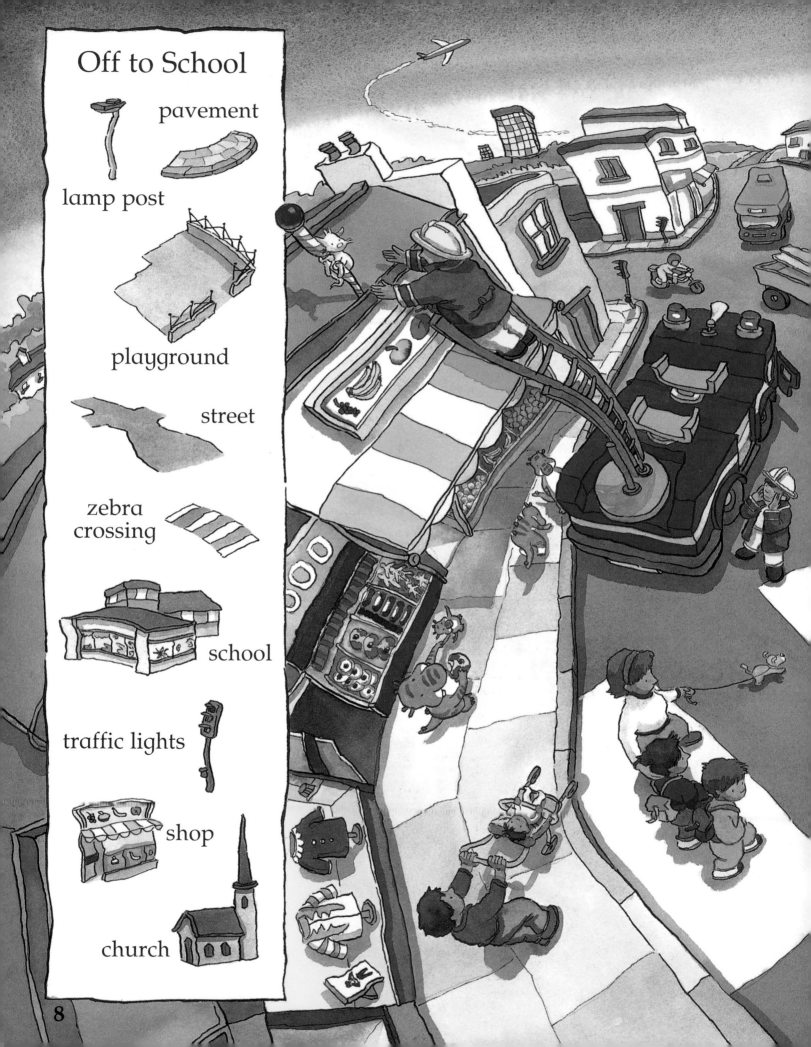

Off to School

pavement

lamp post

playground

street

zebra crossing

school

traffic lights

shop

church

8

bicycle

car

bus

motorbike

fire engine

truck

helicopter

umbulance

plane

9

Our Classroom

school bag

book

lunch box

blackboard

chalk

globe

desk

magnet

bin

10

cassette recorder

cassette

ruler

computer

map

disk

dice

keyboard

mouse

Colour Fun

black

blue

brown

green

grey

orange

pink

purple

red

white

yellow

12

overalls

glue

painting

paintbrush

paints

pencil

paper

scissors

felt pen

easel

13

When I Grow Up

postman

builder

doctor

police officer

vet

footballer

firefighter

bus driver

train driver

pop star

pilot

dancer

diver

cook

astronaut

lifeguard

15

Long Time Ago

Dinosaurs:
200 million years ago

Tyrannosaurus Rex

Stegosaurus

Diplodocus

Triceratops
skeleton

fossil

bone

Stone Age Man:
10,000 years ago

cave

flint

cave painting

fire

Ancient Egyptians:
5,000 years ago

pyramid

sphinx

Pharaoh

Ancient Romans:
2,000 years ago

pottery

coins

soldier

Busy Shopping

trolley

basket

cash register

bread

bun

jam

cereal

potatoes

sausages

spaghetti

milk

yoghurt

cheese

eggs

apple

banana

orange

tomato

carrot

lettuce

19

Monster Lunch

cooker

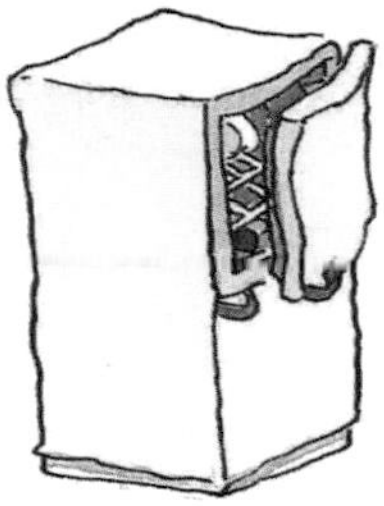

fridge

washing machine

saucepan

iron

cup

bowl

knife

fork

kettle

plate

spoon

saucer

chair

teapot

cushion

sofa

stereo

table

television

video recorder

vacuum cleaner

Time to Play

doll's house

doll

game

racing car

robot

jigsaw puzzle

teddy

train set

drum

guitar

keyboard

microphone

trumpet

recorder

cymbals

bells

tambourine

23

On the Farm

horse

chicken

cock

duck

goose

sheep

goat

pig

cow

24

tractor

stream

bridge

field

forest

hay

hill

scarecrow

25

At the Beach

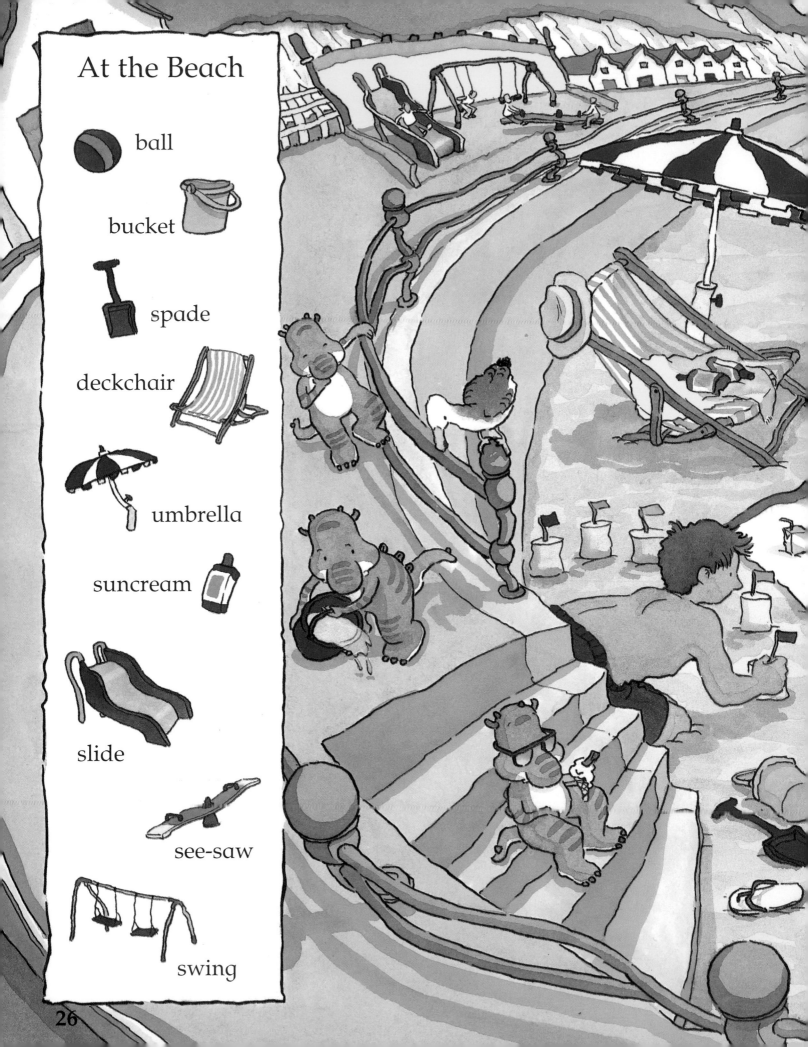

ball

bucket

spade

deckchair

umbrella

suncream

slide

see-saw

swing

ship

lighthouse

sandcastle

seagull

shell

crab

octopus

starfish

seaweed

Birthday Party

birthday card

candle

balloon

present

streamer

party blower

party hat

wand

magician

sweets

sandwich

pizza

ice cream

chocolate

biscuit

straw

drink

cake

Animal Magic

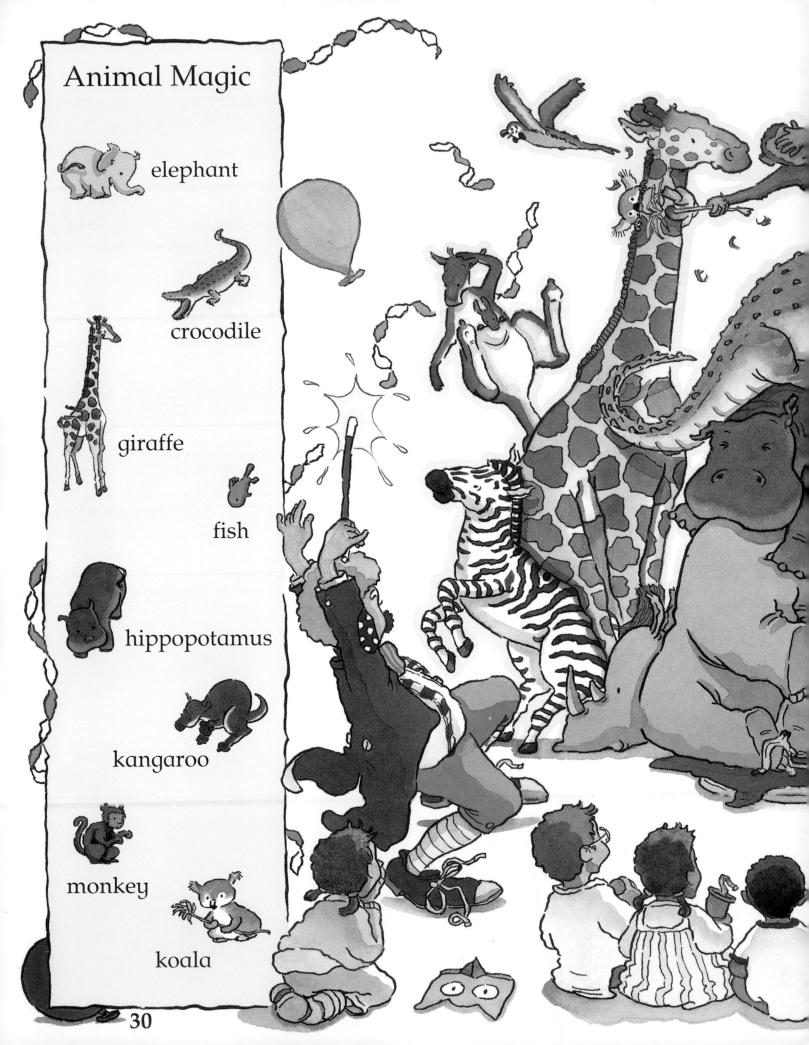

elephant

crocodile

giraffe

fish

hippopotamus

kangaroo

monkey

koala

mouse

walrus

parrot

penguin

tiger

zebra

panda

rhinoceros

In the Bath

 dress

 jacket

 shorts

 shirt

 skirt

 trousers

 jumper

 pants

 shoes

socks

 T-shirt

basin

bath

flannel

mirror

shower

soap

sponge

toilet

toilet paper

toothbrush

toothpaste

towel

Time for Bed

wardrobe

curtains

bedside table

lamp

nightdress

pyjamas

pillow

bed

blanket

chest

storybook

castle

king

queen

genie

magic lamp

dragon

giant

My ABC

A a   ant

B b   bell

C c   caterpillar

D d   dog

E e   egg

F f   fish

G g   goat

H h   helicopter

I i   ink

J j   juggler

K k   king

L l   ladybird

M m   mouse

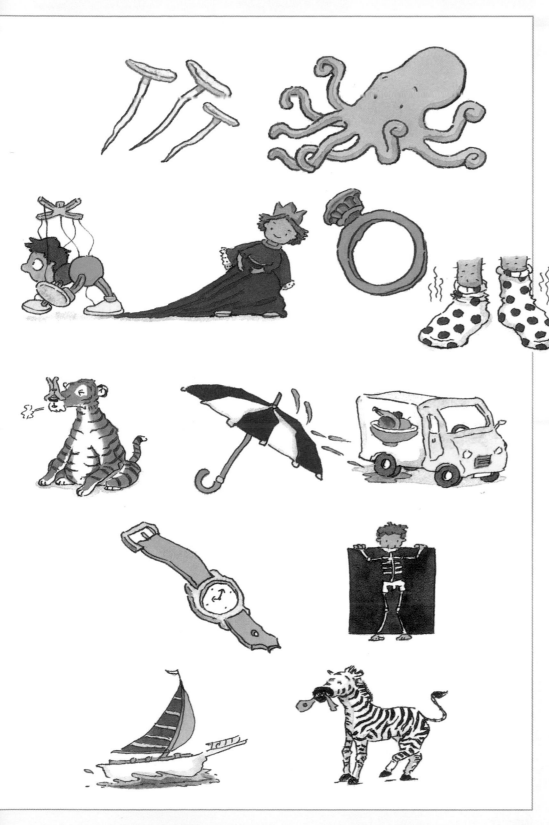

N n   nail

O o   octopus

P p   puppet

Q q   queen

R r   ring

S s   socks

T t   tiger

U u   umbrella

V v   van

W w   watch

X x   X-ray

Y y   yacht

Z z   zebra

Count 123

0 zero 1 one 2 two 3 three

4 four 5 five 6 six 7 seven

8 eight 9 nine 10 ten

first second third

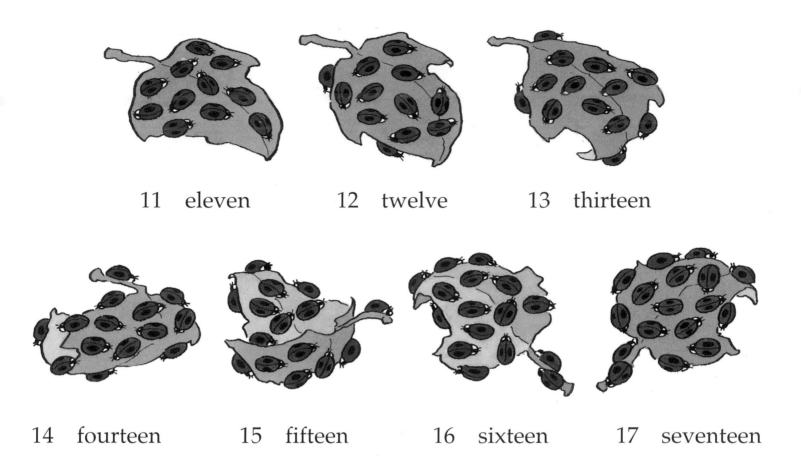

11 eleven   12 twelve   13 thirteen

14 fourteen   15 fifteen   16 sixteen   17 seventeen

18 eighteen   19 nineteen   20 twenty

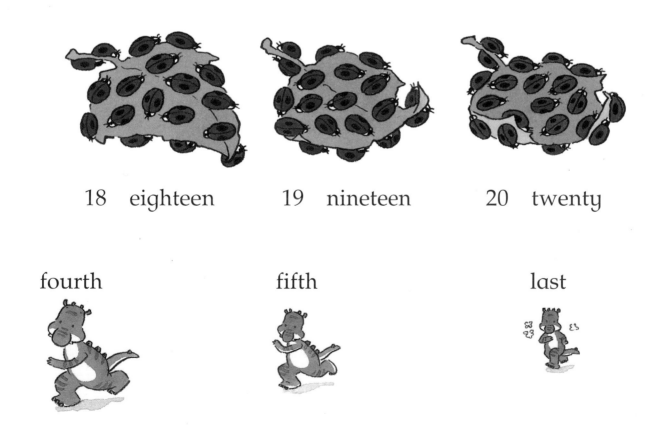

fourth   fifth   last

Shapes

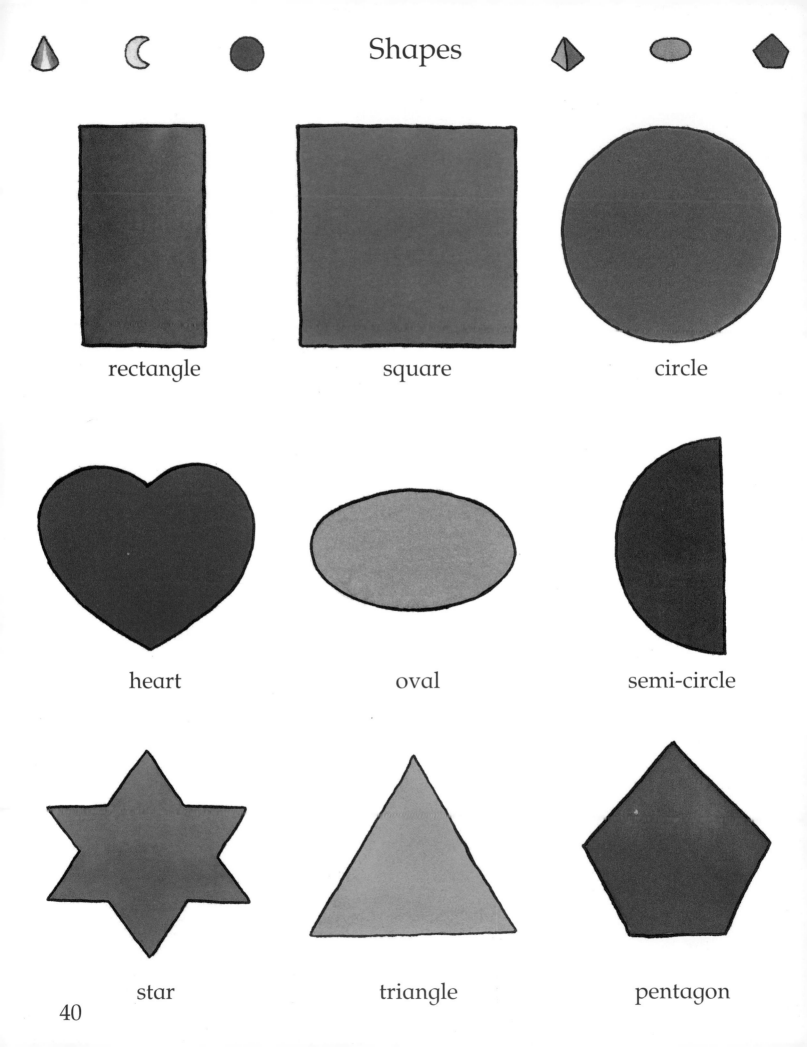

rectangle

square

circle

heart

oval

semi-circle

star

triangle

pentagon

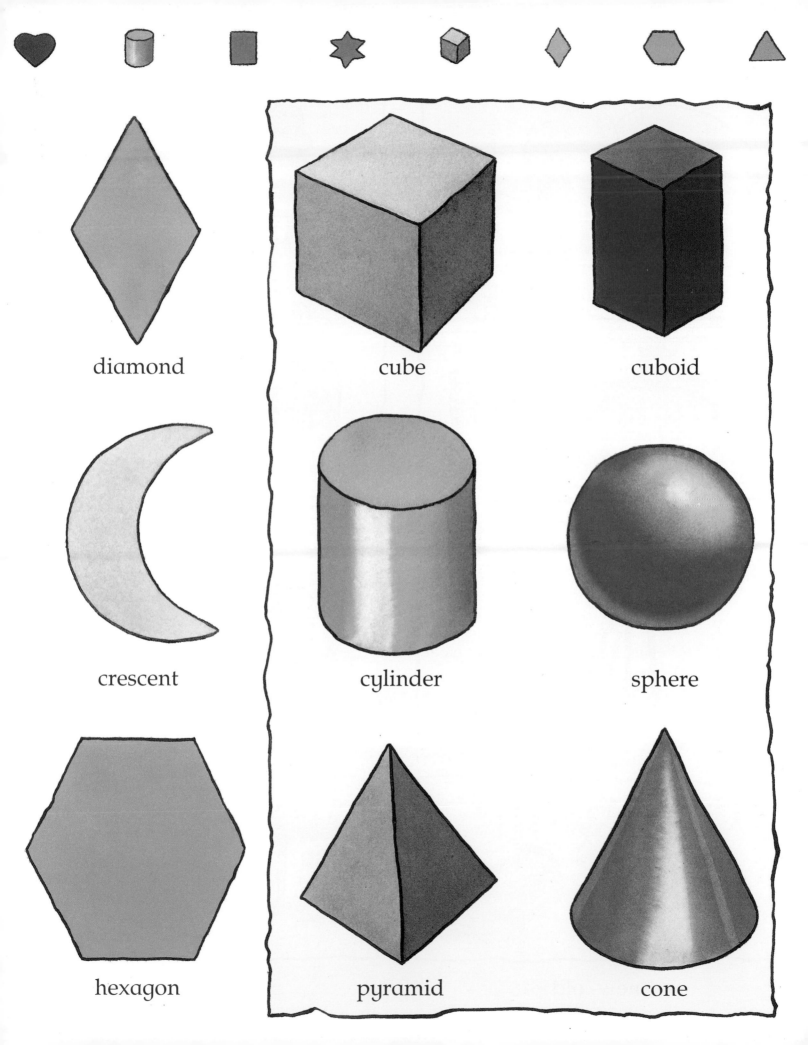

diamond

cube

cuboid

crescent

cylinder

sphere

hexagon

pyramid

cone

Opposites

big/small

clean/dirty

fat/thin

full/empty

high/low

hot/cold

new/old

open/closed

dark/light

fast/slow

happy/sad

heavy/light

long/short

more/less

same/different

wet/dry

cloudy

sunny

rainy

snowy

windy

foggy

eight o'clock

ten o'clock

twelve noon

two o'clock

four o'clock

six o'clock

Index

ambulance	9	cave painting	17	door	6	game	22
ant	36	cereal	18	dragon	35	garage	6
apple	19	chair	19	dress	32	gate	6
arm	4	chalk	10	drink	29	genie	35
astronaut	15	cheek	5	drum	23	giant	35
		cheese	19	dry	43	giraffe	30
back	4	chest (body)	4	duck	24	girl	5
ball	26	chest (furniture)	34	dustbin	6	globe	10
balloon	28	chicken	24			glue	13
banana	19	chimney	6			goat	24, 36
basin	33	chin	5	ear	5	goose	24
basket	18	chocolate	29	easel	13	green	12
bath	33	church	8	egg	36	grey	12
bed	34	circle	40	eggs	19	guitar	23
bedside table	34	clean	42	eight	38		
bell	36	closed	42	eighteen	39		
bells	23	cloudy	44	elbow	4	hair	4
bicycle	9	cock	24	elephant	30	hand	4
big	42	coins	17	eleven	39	happy	43
bin	10	cold	42	empty	42	hay	25
birthday card	28	computer	11	eye	5	head	4
biscuit	29	cone	41			heart	40
black	12	cook	15			heavy	43
blackboard	10	cooker	20	face	5	helicopter	9, 36
blanket	34	cow	24	fast	43	hexagon	41
blue	12	crab	27	fat	42	high	42
bone	16	crescent	41	felt pen	13	hill	25
book	10	crocodile	30	fence	6	hippopotamus	30
bottom	4	cube	41	field	25	horse	24
bowl	20	cuboid	41	fifteen	39	hot	42
boy	5	cup	20	fifth	39		
bread	18	curtains	34	finger	4		
bridge	25	cushion	21	fire	17	ice cream	29
brown	12	cylinder	41	fire engine	9	ink	36
bucket	26	cymbals	23	firefighter	14	iron	20
builder	14			first	38		
bun	18			fish	30, 36	jacket	32
bus	9	dancer	15	five	38	jam	18
bus driver	14	dark	43	flannel	33	jigsaw puzzle	22
		deckchair	26	flint	17	juggler	36
cake	29	desk	10	flower	7	jumper	32
candle	28	diamond	41	foggy	44		
car	9	dice	11	foot	4	kangaroo	30
carrot	19	different	43	footballer	14	kettle	20
cash register	18	Diplodocus	16	forest	25	keyboard (music)	23
cassette	11	dirty	42	fork	20	keyboard (PC)	11
cassette recorder	11	disk	11	fossil	16	king	35, 36
castle	35	diver	15	four	38	knee	4
cat	7	doctor	14	fourteen	39	knife	20
caterpillar	36	dog	7, 36	fourth	39	koala	30
cave	17	doll	22	fridge	20		
		doll's house	22	full	42	ladybird	36
						lamp	34

lamp post 8
last 39
leaf 7
leg 4
less 43
letters 7
lettuce 19
lifeguard 15
light 43
lighthouse 27
long 43
low 42
lunch box 10

magic lamp 35
magician 28
magnet 10
map 11
microphone 23
milk 19
mirror 33
monkey 30
more 43
motorbike 9
mouse (animal) 31,36
mouse (PC) 11
mouth 5

nail 37
neck 5
new 42
nightdress 34
nine 38
nineteen 39
nose 5

octopus 27, 37
old 42
one 38
open 42
orange (colour) 12
orange (fruit) 19
oval 40
overalls 13

paintbrush 13
painting 13
paints 13
panda 31
pants 32
paper 13
parrot 31
party blower 28
party hat 28
pavement 8
pencil 13

penguin 31
pentagon 40
Pharoah 17
pig 24
pillow 34
pilot 15
pink 12
pizza 29
plane 9
plate 20
playground 8
police officer 14
pop star 15
post bag 7
postman 14
potatoes 18
pottery 17
present 28
puppet 37
purple 12
pyjamas 34
pyramid (Egypt) 17
pyramid (shape) 41

queen 35, 37

rabbit 7
racing car 22
rainy 44
recorder 23
rectangle 40
red 12
rhinoceros 31
ring 37
robot 22
roof 6
ruler 11

sad 43
same 43
sandcastle 27
sandwich 29
saucepan 20
saucer 21
sausages 18
scarecrow 25
school 8
school bag 10
scissors 13
seagull 27
seaweed 27
second 38
see-saw 26
semi-circle 40
seven 38
seventeen 39

sheep 24
shell 27
ship 27
shirt 32
shoes 32
shop 8
short 43
shorts 32
shoulders 4
shower 33
six 38
sixteen 39
skeleton 16
skirt 32
slide 26
slow 43
small 42
snail 7
snowy 44
soap 33
socks 32, 37
sofa 21
soldier 17
spade 26
spaghetti 18
sphere 41
sphinx 17
spider 7
sponge 33
spoon 21
square 40
stairs 6
star 40
starfish 27
Stegosaurus 16
stereo 21
storybook 35
straw 29
stream 25
streamer 28
street 8
suncream 26
sunny 44
sweets 29
swing 26

T-shirt 32
table 21
tambourine 23
teapot 21
teddy 22
teeth 5
television 21
ten 38
thin 42
third 38

thirteen 39
three 38
tiger 31, 37
time 45
toe 4
toilet 33
toilet paper 33
tomato 19
tongue 5
toothbrush 33
toothpaste 33
towel 33
tractor 25
traffic lights 8
train driver 15
train set 22
tree 7
triangle 40
Triceratops 16
trolley 18
trousers 32
truck 9
trumpet 23
tummy 4
twelve 39
twenty 39
two 38
Tyrannosaurus Rex 16

umbrella 26, 37

vacuum cleaner 21
van 37
vet 14
video recorder 21

walrus 31
wand 28
wardrobe 34
washing machine 20
watch 37
wet 43
white 12
window 6
windy 44

X-ray 37

yacht 37
yellow 12
yoghurt 19

zebra 31, 37
zebra crossing 8
zero 38

47